Dachshunds in Moccasins

Written by: Nadine Poper

Illustrated by: Michele Wallace

For Ryan, Adam, Aaron, and Russ ~N.P.

For David, Jesse, and Julia ~M.W.

Dachshunds
in
Moccasins

Hamchinpolelly awoke to the sound of barking dogs. It was never quiet where he lived except in the middle of the night when all the other dogs were sleeping.

This morning was no different. Hamchinpolelly would wait for the kennel worker to open the outdoor pen so he could walk out into the fresh air.

And he would wait with his shoes on.
He would wait for the people to come.
Maybe this would be the day.

Many people, all day long, would come in
and out of the kennel looking for their new dog.

His family needed to move away
to a place where he couldn't go.

They had bought him dog booties, but
they were tattered and worn out by now.

He never took them off.

Hamchinpolelly was a
dachshund
who did NOT like

his feet
to be cold.

Hamchinpolelly ate quickly that morning so he wouldn't miss anyone coming by his kennel to look at him.

Outside he went and waited.

And waited while people walked by.

Some would stop and read the card on his cage.

"Hamchinpolelly? That is a strange name, and look, he's got booties on," they would say and walk on by.

"Hamchinpolelly? I can barely even say that name," said another.

"Looks like this dachshund needs a new pair of dog booties," remarked one more.

"How did he get that name?" from still another.

Finally, after what seemed like hours, a young boy
was standing in front of Hamchinpolelly's door.

The boy didn't walk by. He didn't say anything about
Hamchinpolelly's name or his booties. The boy stared
at Hamchinpolelly and Hamchinpolelly stared at the
boy.

"Hey Mom!" the boy shouted. "What about this one?"

A woman walked up to the kennel door and peered in. She then looked at the card on the wall.

"Hamchinpolelly? What kind of name is that? And I've never seen a dog in shoes before."

But she could see how much her son loved this dog, and she could see the dog's gentle ways.

After the paperwork was signed, the boy carried his new dog to the car and put him in a crate to keep him safe.

The boy checked the dog's booties because he didn't want his dog's feet to get cold.

Over the next few weeks, everything was good with Hamchinpolelly and his new family.

They called him Ham for short.

The boy would take Ham for long walks in the park, and Ham would snuggle with the family watching movies with his booties on because he didn't want his feet to get cold.

One such day when the family was watching TV,
something caught Ham's eye.

What was on Dad's feet?

They looked soft.
They looked cozy.
And they looked like they would keep his feet
from being cold.

When the movie ended, Ham followed
everyone to bed,

but he watched Dad closely.

Later that night while everyone slept, Ham crept into the bedroom where he saw THEM.

To his delight, these shoes were soft.
They were cozy.
And they would keep his feet from being cold!

Ham slipped his left paw inside Dad's slipper,

and off to his bed he went.

The next morning Dad came downstairs
looking for his other moccasin, and when
he saw Ham,

Dad placed the other moccasin on his other paw.

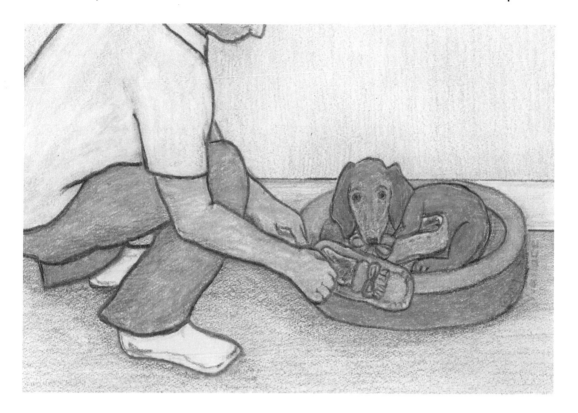

Hamchinpolelly loved his new discovery,
though sometimes
he would trip…
he would stumble…
he would fall down.

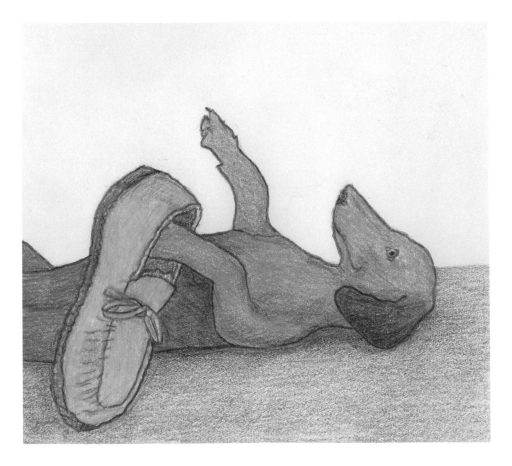

But the smile would never leave his face.
These two large moccasins looked out of place
with his other booties.
And they NEVER stayed on his feet for very long.

Ham would wear his moccasins outside.
He would wear his moccasins inside.
He would wear them to sleep and to play.

One time the boy wanted to play a game he called
"Hide the Moccasin",
but Ham did not like that game very much.

Seeing how much Hamchinpolelly loved Dad's moccasins, it was decided that Ham needed some of his own size.

After a time, Hamchinpolelly's size began to change.

"Mom, do you think we are feeding Ham too much food?" the boy asked one day.

"No, I don't believe so. We are feeding him just the way the lady at the pet store told us to," was her reply.

But as the weeks went by, Ham's size was definitely changing.

And one morning the family awoke to a wonderful surprise!

"I guess Ham is a girl dachshund," said the boy.

The boy and his mom got to work right away on twenty very tiny moccasins…

...because
they didn't
want the
pups' feet
to get
cold.